For Sarah and Paul
J.S.

For David Moss, Peter,

Mum and Dad

T.L.

Text © 1996 by Julie Sykes
Pictures © 1996 by Tanya Linch
All rights reserved
First published in England by Magi Publications, 1996
Printed and bound in Italy by Grafiche AZ, Verona
First American edition, 1996
Library of Congress Cataloging-in-Publication Data
Sykes, Julie.
This and that / by Julie Sykes ; pictures by Tanya Linch.
—1st American ed.
p. cm.
[1. Cats—Fiction. 2. Domestic animals—Fiction.]
I. Linch, Tanya, ill. II. Title.
PZ7.S98325Th 1996 [E]—dc20 95-21259 CIP AC

Farrar, Straus and Giroux

New York

This and That

by Julie Sykes

Pictures by Tanya Linch

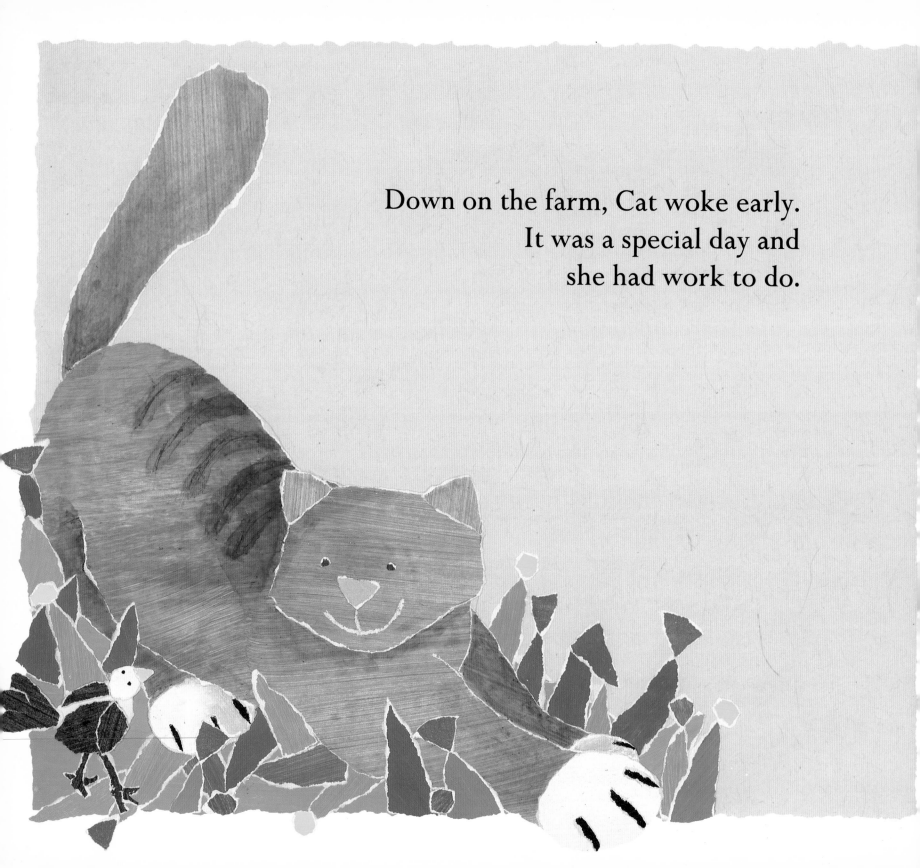

Down on the farm, Cat woke early.
It was a special day and
she had work to do.

Horse was grazing in the field when
Cat jumped onto the fence.

"Hello, Horse," said Cat. "May I borrow
your stable?"
Horse didn't use his stable in the summer
because he liked to sleep outside.
"Yes," he neighed. "What will
you use it for?"
"This and that," purred the cat.

Pig was rolling in his sty
when Cat leapt onto the wall.

"Hello, Pig," said Cat. "May I have some
of your straw?"
The farmer had just made Pig's bed.
The straw was clean and fresh, and there
was plenty of it.
"Help yourself," grunted Pig. "What's it for?"
"This and that," purred the cat.

Goat was playing in the yard when
Cat hopped on the gate and meowed.

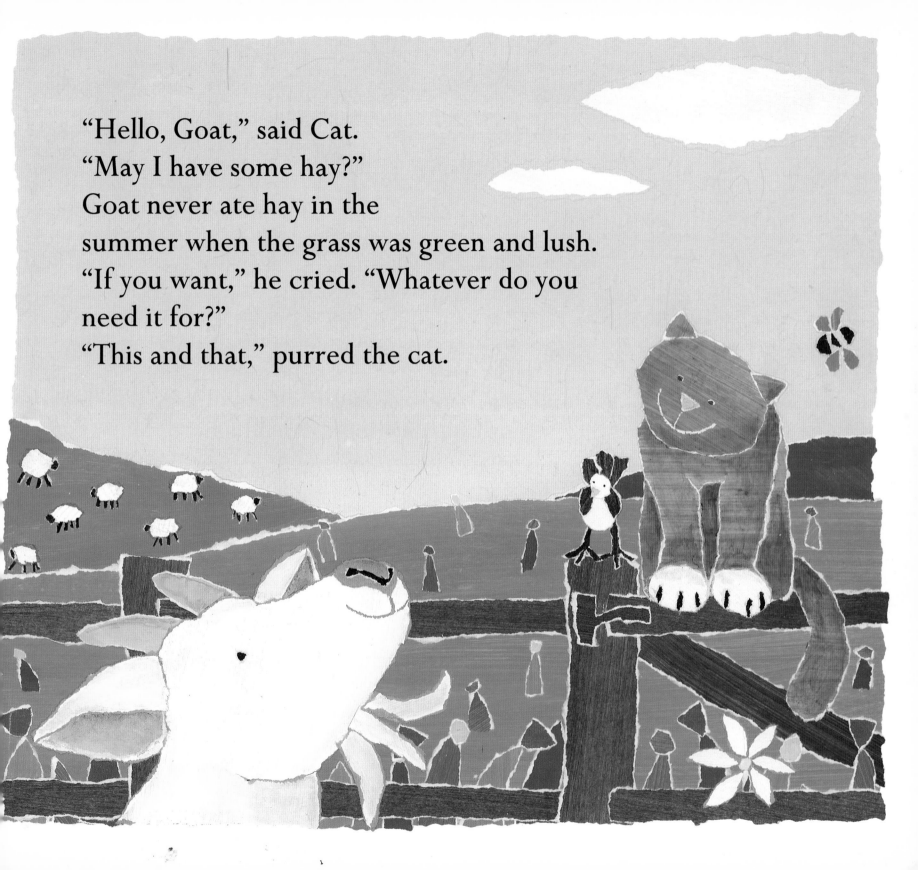

"Hello, Goat," said Cat.
"May I have some hay?"
Goat never ate hay in the
summer when the grass was green and lush.
"If you want," he cried. "Whatever do you
need it for?"
"This and that," purred the cat.

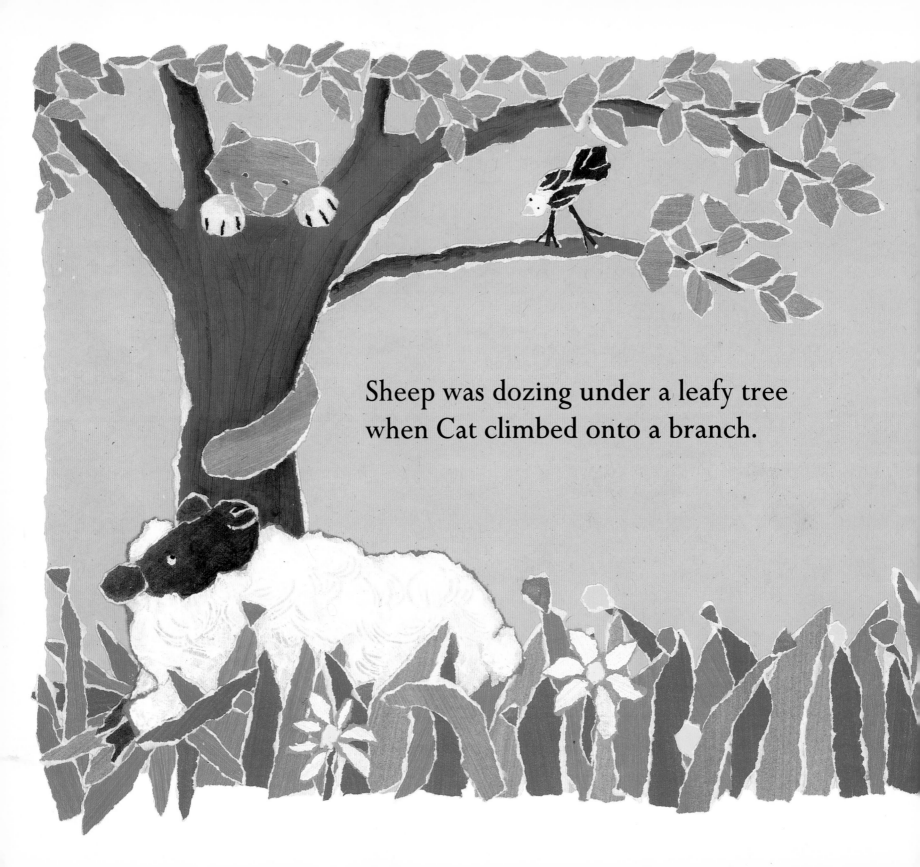

Sheep was dozing under a leafy tree
when Cat climbed onto a branch.

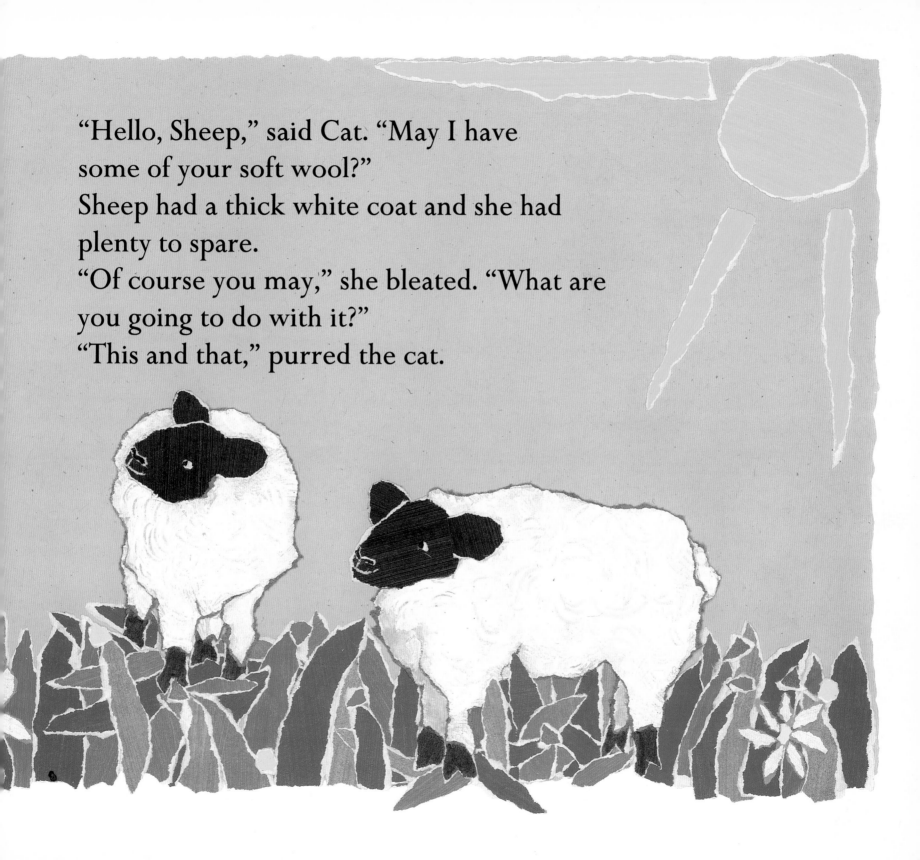

"Hello, Sheep," said Cat. "May I have some of your soft wool?"
Sheep had a thick white coat and she had plenty to spare.
"Of course you may," she bleated. "What are you going to do with it?"
"This and that," purred the cat.

Hen was scratching for grain when Cat leapt on top of the henhouse.

"Hello, Hen," said Cat.
"May I have a few of your
feathers?"
Hen stopped scratching and
cocked her head curiously.
"You may," she clucked.
"But whatever for?"
"This and that," purred the cat.

Cow was drinking from the stream
when Cat joined her on the bank.

"Hello, Cow," said Cat. "May I have a few hairs from your tail?"
Cow had a long tail with a hairy tip for swatting flies.
"Yes," she mooed. "What are you going to do with them?"
"This and that," purred the cat.

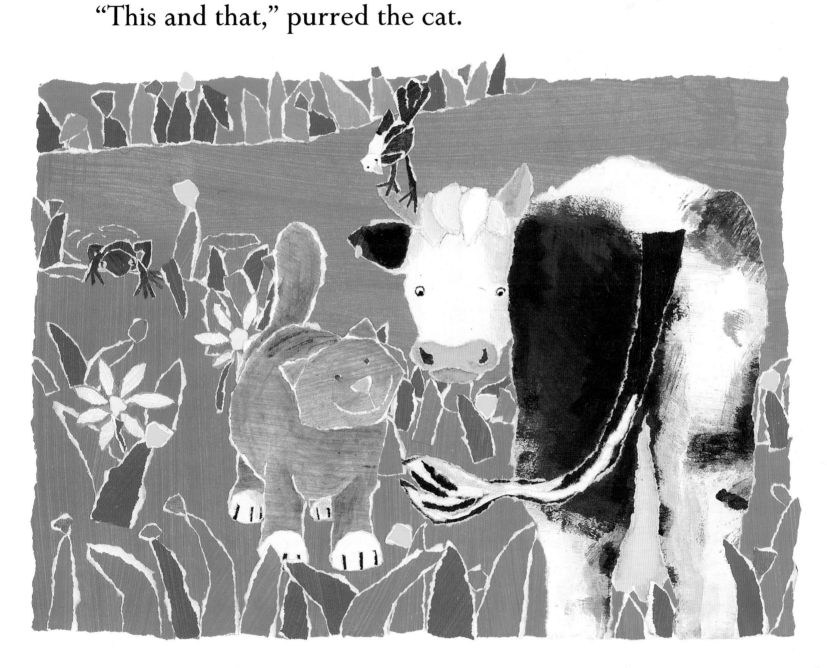

Donkey was looking for thistles
when Cat jumped on his back.

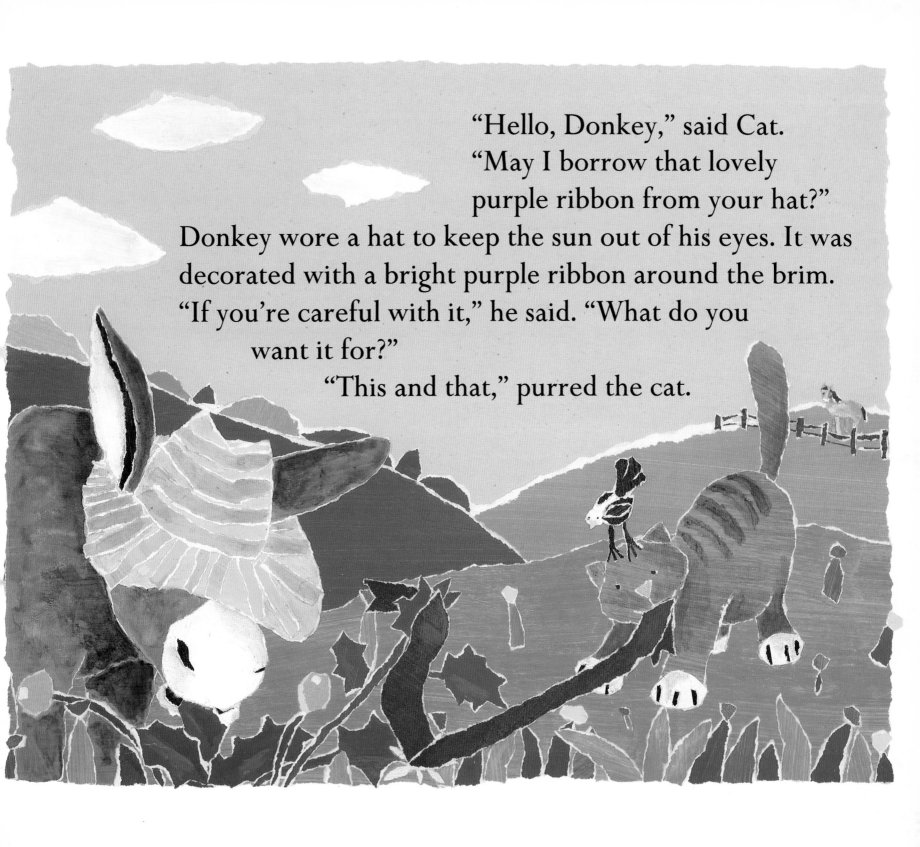

"Hello, Donkey," said Cat.
"May I borrow that lovely
purple ribbon from your hat?"
Donkey wore a hat to keep the sun out of his eyes. It was
decorated with a bright purple ribbon around the brim.
"If you're careful with it," he said. "What do you
want it for?"
"This and that," purred the cat.

The animals thought Cat was behaving strangely.
"What does she want with all our things?" clucked Hen.
"Perhaps she's moving house," mooed Cow.
"No," grunted Pig. "Cats don't like moving."
"Let's follow her," brayed Donkey.

The animals all hid in
the yard, and when Cat
appeared they tiptoed
after her.

Cat went inside the stable, and the
animals followed silently behind.

In one corner they saw . . .

. . . two little kittens!

They were inside a nest
made from hay and straw.
It was lined with
Sheep's wool,
hair from Cow's tail,
and feathers from Hen.
It was decorated with
Donkey's pretty purple
ribbon.

"What a lovely surprise,"
neighed Horse.
"They're beautiful," said Goat.
"So that's what you needed our
things for!" exclaimed Sheep.
Leaning over the huge nest,
Donkey asked, "What are
they called?"
Cat sighed. "I don't know,
I can't decide. What do you think?"
The animals looked at each other.

Then together they

neighed and grunted,

bleated and clucked,

hee-hawed and mooed,

"WE KNOW . . ."